The Queen Bakes a Pie

By Julie Kelly

Illustrations by Pat Tkachyk

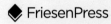 FriesenPress

Suite 300 - 990 Fort St
Victoria, BC, V8V 3K2
Canada

www.friesenpress.com

ISBN
978-1-5255-7353-8 (Hardcover)
978-1-5255-7354-5 (Paperback)
978-1-5255-7355-2 (eBook)

1. JUVENILE FICTION, SOCIAL ISSUES, SELF-ESTEEM & SELF-RELIANCE

Distributed to the trade by The Ingram Book Company

For my princess, Emersen,
your kind soul and determination inspire me every day.

May you always know your strength and that you are loved.

Once upon a time in a big, beautiful castle in a faraway land, way up on a hill, deep in the forest, lived a brave and kind princess named Emersen. She lived with her mom, the queen; her dad, the king; and her miniature pet dragon named Prince.

One day, while Princess Emersen was playing fetch outside with Prince, the postman arrived in a horse-drawn carriage.

"Good morning," said the postman.

"Good morning," replied the princess.

"I have a very important letter to deliver to the queen. Is she home?"

"Yes!" said the princess with excitement. "I can bring it to her. She's just over there, tending to her flowers." The princess pointed to the queen, who was kneeling on the grass, pulling weeds from around her daffodils.

"Are you sure?" the postman asked, looking at her curiously. "It is very important."

The postman held the letter out in his hand, and the princess reached up to grab it.

"Of course!" she said with enthusiasm. "I am very responsible." And with a flash, the princess took the letter and ran to bring it to her mom.

"Thank you!" she yelled to the postman as she dashed away with Prince close on her heels, lugging his favourite toy in his mouth.

"Mom," shouted Princess Emersen, "this letter just arrived for you!" Emersen handed her mom the letter from the postman and watched eagerly as she opened it.

"What does it say?" she shouted.

"Be patient, my dear," replied the queen as she pulled out a bright pink card with orange polka dots on it. "It's an invitation to the annual Queen's Baking Competition," said the queen.

"Wow!" shouted the princess.

"The invitation says that the competition is in three days at the Community Hall building," read the queen. "But I don't think that I'm going to be entering a pie this year, sweetheart," the queen said sadly.

"How come?" the princess asked.

"It takes a lot of time and hard work to bake a great pie. Plus, I don't know if any of my recipes will turn out good enough to win a competition."

"But Mom," exclaimed Princess Emersen, "you have always wanted to enter the competition. You will do great. You are a queen!"

"Let me think about it," the queen replied. "Now come on, it's time to head inside."

Emersen and Prince were busy playing games in the princess's room when she suddenly had an idea.

"Princey!" she shouted. "We should go and tell the king about mom's competition. I'm sure he will know how we can get mom to enter."

Prince quickly gathered up his toys, trying to fit all of them in his mouth at once, and he followed the princess down the hallway to speak with the king, who was enjoying a new book in the library.

"Hello, Dad," said the princess.

"Well, hello, my dear," said the king, "and hello to you too, Prince." The miniature dragon shook his tail with so much excitement that his toys fell out of his mouth and landed in front of him.

"You are such a silly dragon," laughed the king, and he gave Prince a pat on his head.

"How is your day going, Princess?" asked the king.

"Pretty good," said the princess, "but I could use your help."

"With what?" asked the king.

"Well, today mom was invited to the Queen's Baking Competition, but she doesn't think she will be able to enter. And I really think she should," said the princess.

"Hmm," replied the king, "that is very kind and thoughtful of you to say. I think she should enter as well. She's always talking about how baking the best pie at the competition has been a dream of hers. Let me see what I can do," said the king.

Then the king leaned down and kissed the princess on the forehead. Prince stretched up high and tried to get a kiss from the king too, but instead, he got another loving pat on the head.

"You two run along now," said the king. "I have a few phone calls to make. I will see you at dinner."

Later that evening, while the family was sitting around the dining room table about to eat, there was a knock at the door.

"Who could that be?" asked the queen.

"I arranged for a special visitor to join us for dinner tonight," said the king.

At that moment, Prince's tail began to wag with excitement as Grandma walked into the dining room.

"Hello, everyone," she announced with a smile.

"Grandma," Princess Emersen shouted, "I'm so happy to see you!"

"Hello, sweetheart, I am very happy to see you as well! I have been called here on very important royal business," Grandma said as she sat down next to the princess.

"What is your important business?" asked the queen.

The king was quick to answer. "I called her and asked her to come and help. I know that you have dreamed about entering the Queen's Baking Competition for many years. You do so much for all of us, and it is time that you have something special of your own. We are going to help you bake the best pie you can bake!"

"That is awfully nice of you all," said the queen. "But I don't think I can do it. It's a lot of work, and there are other queens who have been baking way longer than I have. Plus, I don't even have a recipe to use."

"That is why I am here!" exclaimed Grandma. "I have brought you my top-secret, first-place-winning pie recipe! And a map."

"A map?" asked the queen.

"Yes," replied Grandma. "In order to bake this pie, we will need to go on a quest to get all of the special ingredients."

"A quest?" asked Princess Emersen. "That sounds fun!"

"Oh, it will be an adventure for sure," said Grandma. "It can get tricky though. That is why we must all go together and work as a team. And we have to be quick, because the competition is only a few short days away."

"All right," replied the queen, "I will do it. I will go on a quest and enter the competition."

"Yay!" everyone cheered with excitement.

"Now, we should all get a good night's sleep," said the king. "We will be leaving bright and early tomorrow morning."

The next morning, just as the sun was peeking out above the trees, the royal family set out on their quest, with Prince soaring eagerly at their side.

The queen reviewed Grandma's recipe, pulling it out of a wicker basket she had brought from the castle kitchen. "We need to find sugar, flour, and blueberries," read the queen. "We can store all of our ingredients safely in this basket, along with our map."

"Where are we going first?" asked Princess Emersen.

Grandma looked at her map and said, "First we must travel down the hill behind the castle, then turn left at the large rock, and follow the path through the forest until we reach *Sugar Flake Mountain*."

"Where do we go after that?" asked the princess.

"I'm not sure," said Grandma. "It is a magical map. We will only be able to see where to go next after we have the sugar."

"Let's get started," said the king. "We haven't a moment to waste."

The royal family carefully followed the trail on the map until they reached the edge of the forest. The air became cool, and as a gentle breeze swirled through the sky, it tickled Prince's nose, which caused him to sneeze a little bit of fire. In front of them stood a huge mountain.

"I think we've arrived at *Sugar Flake Mountain*," announced the queen.

"Look at all the snow up on top," Princess Emersen said, amazed.

"That's not snow," said Grandma. "Those are sugar flakes. The recipe says we need to collect six sugar flakes, but we have to be careful not to let them fall apart. They are very delicate."

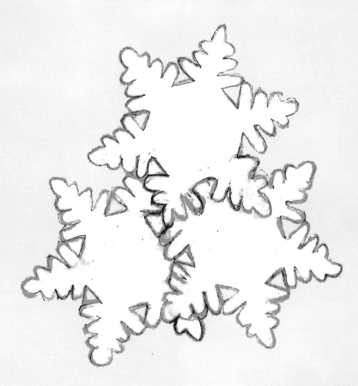

"How will we get to the top?" asked the princess.

"I think we need to climb to the top," replied the king.

Together, everyone looked at the mountain. It was too steep to climb, and even if they did get to the top, how would they get down without crushing the sugar flakes?

"I have an idea!" said Princess Emersen. "I will ride on Prince's back to the top of the mountain. When we get to the top, I'll have him fly around really fast to create some wind. The wind should set enough sugar flakes free to float down to the ground," she said excitedly.

"What a clever idea; you are so smart," said the queen. "But that sounds awfully dangerous."

"Mom, there is no other way. I am strong and will hold on tight," Princess Emersen said.

"Okay," said the queen, "I know you can do this. Just please be careful." The queen gave Princess Emersen a kiss on her forehead, and the Princess climbed onto the pet dragon's back.

"You'll have to move quickly once you get to the top," said the king. "We cannot have Prince blow out any fire, or he will melt all of the sugar flakes."

"Come on, Princey!" shouted Emersen, and with a flash they were up in the air, soaring higher and higher in the sky. Soon they were out of sight. Everyone waited nervously for their return when suddenly it began to snow. Sugar flakes were falling gently to the ground. The queen pulled out the basket and very carefully caught six sugar flakes.

"We did it!" Princess Emersen shouted, as she and Prince landed safely back on the ground.

"Great job! We are so proud of you!" they all said, cheering and clapping for Emersen.

"And great job, Prince!" said the king as he gave him a scratch behind his ear.

"Where to next?" Emersen asked while pointing to the map in her grandmother's hands.

Everyone gathered together to look at the magical map. Just like Grandma had said it would, the map revealed the next place.

"It says to head east, to the *Great Wheat Field*," Grandma said while looking at the map. "We need to collect six bundles of wheat."

"All right, let's go," said the king as he turned to lead the way with Prince by his side.

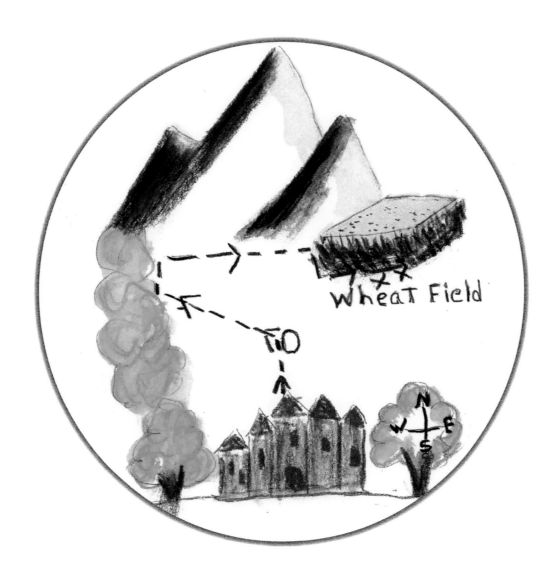

Together, the royal family travelled to the prairies. The ground became flat, and they could see a field full of tall wheat plants in the distance. In front of them appeared a rushing river, with a bridge hanging over top.

"That bridge doesn't look too good," Grandma said.

The bridge was made of wooden planks and rope, but it was falling apart.

"Oh no!" exclaimed Emersen. "How will we get across?"

"Don't worry," said the king. He grabbed some rope that was lying on the ground. "We can fix it. We just need to reattach the loose planks so we can walk across safely. Someone needs to come on the bridge with me to hold the planks in place while I secure the rope."

"I'll do it," replied the queen.

"You're so brave, Mom," Emersen said proudly.

"Thanks, honey," said the queen, "I saw how brave you were at the mountain, and now it is my turn."

The king and queen ventured out onto the bridge. They worked together to put every plank back in place. When they were finished repairing the bridge, they crossed the river safely and continued on their way.

The wheat was a beautiful golden brown and was growing much taller than they had thought.

"Wow, I could get lost in there," Emersen said as she looked out onto the vast wheat field.

"That is why we must stay together," replied the king. "That goes for you too, Prince. No wandering away." Prince turned back to look at the king when he heard his name. He had noticed some footprints in the dirt and was trying to sneak off into the field to follow them.

"Come on, boy!" Emersen shouted. Prince quickly ran to her side, giving up on his plan to go exploring.

"This wheat will be turned into the flour you need to make your pie crust," Grandma explained.

Together, Emersen and her family grabbed hold of a plant and began to harvest the wheat until they had all six bundles needed for the queen's recipe. Once the wheat was safely stored in the basket, Grandma pulled out the magical map to see where they needed to travel next for their final ingredient.

The map showed their third and final destination. They were to continue travelling east, until they reached the large red and white lighthouse, where they would find the *giggling blueberry bushes.*

Side by side, the royal family walked and walked and walked until they could hear waves crashing and seagulls singing. When they looked up, there stood a giant red and white lighthouse at the edge of a cliff.

"I think we have arrived at our final destination," Grandma said excitedly.

"But where are the giggling blueberries?" asked Princess Emersen. "All I see are those bushes, but they don't have any berries on them." Princess Emersen pointed to a bunch of dark green bushes surrounding the lighthouse.

"Let's get a closer look," said the king.

They walked closer to the bushes and noticed hundreds of large blueberries hiding beneath the leaves.

"The recipe says we need ten of these blueberries," said the queen. She leaned over to pick one, but the leaves suddenly moved to block the berries. "That was strange," said the queen curiously. "I can't seem to pick any of these berries."

"Maybe we have to make the blueberry patch giggle," suggested Grandma.

"That sounds silly," said Emersen.

"It certainly does," said the queen, "but it's worth a try. The sun is starting to go down, and we need to make it back to the castle before dark."

"What should we do?" asked the king.

"I know a knock-knock joke," replied the princess.

"Okay, let's hear it," said Grandma.

Princess Emersen told a joke, and when she was done, the bushes started to move a little.

"It's working!" squealed the queen. "Keep going!"

Together, everyone took turns telling jokes and silly stories. They remembered the time when Prince was a baby and used to trip over his tail when he carried too many toys in his mouth. As their laughter grew louder, the giggling blueberry bushes shook more and more until the blueberries began to bounce up and down and fall to the ground. They were the size of baseballs! Everyone gathered what they could, as the berries tried to jump away from them. They ran after the ones rolling away. Prince tried to help too, but he just ended up eating them—his mouth was all purple from the blueberry juice.

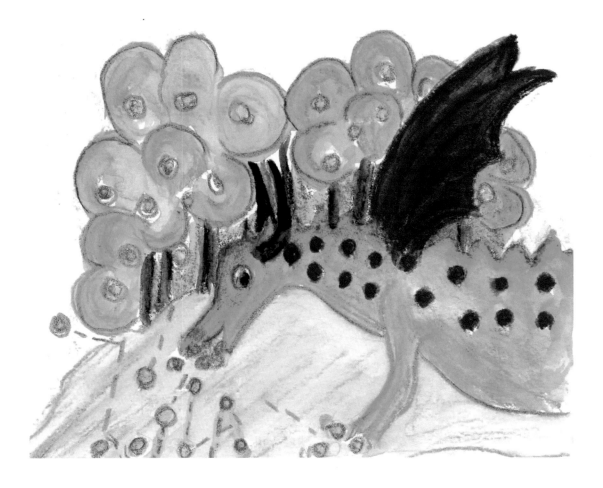

Finally, after they had collected all ten large blueberries and safely placed them in the basket, it was time to head home. They had found all of the magical ingredients the queen needed to bake her pie.

Grandma took one last look at the map and announced that there was a shortcut back to the castle. She took Emersen by the hand and lead the way back home, where their journey had begun.

The royal family was tired by the time they got back to the castle. But there was still a lot of work to be done—the baking competition was tomorrow!

"Let us help you," said the king.

"I can bring all of the special ingredients we found today into the kitchen," announced Emersen excitedly.

"Don't forget this," Grandma said, handing Emersen a bag of cinnamon. "You cannot bake a winning pie without cinnamon."

"Thank you all so much," said the queen. "Thank you for joining me on that big journey today. Your support and encouragement mean so much." The queen leaned down and gave the princess a kiss on her forehead. "My sweet Princess, I am especially proud of you. You are so smart, and you showed such bravery and courage today. I love you so much."

"I love you too, Mom," Princess Emersen said, smiling.

"Well, shall we get started?" asked the queen, with her magic recipe in hand.

While the rest of the castle was quiet, and day turned to night, the royal family was busy in the kitchen. First they ground the prairie wheat to make flour, making a white, floury mess all over themselves. Then the queen used the flour to make her pie crust. She baked one pie crust after another, changing things just a little each time, until finally a pie crust came out fluffy and crisp.

Then they mixed the giggling blueberries with the sugar flakes and cinnamon to make the pie filling. Minutes turned to hours as the queen worked hard with her helpers by her side to bake the perfect pie.

Finally, she pulled her finished masterpiece out of the oven and set it on the counter to cool. Then she announced proudly, "I have done my very best. Come along everyone."

One after the other, they left the kitchen, including Prince, who had fallen asleep at their feet. The queen then turned off the kitchen light. "Tomorrow is another big day," she said, "and we all need to get some rest."

The next morning, the sun was shining, and the entire castle was buzzing with excitement. It was competition day!

Everyone got dressed up and again ventured out to support the queen, who was proudly carrying her pie.

Just as they were approaching the front steps of the Community Hall building, a beautiful woman with long, dark hair and a long dress appeared.

"Excuse me," said the woman to the queen, "I can't help but notice that you are entering the baking competition today."

"Yes, I am," the queen said with a polite smile.

"I heard the competition is pretty tough this year. Are you sure your pie is good enough?" the woman asked.

"You look familiar? Have I seen you before?" the queen asked the woman.

"I don't believe so," said the woman as she pulled out a tiny vile of sprinkles. "Can I interest you in some magic sprinkles? I guarantee they will make you a first-place winner."

The queen paused to think. Now she was beginning to doubt if her pie was any good.

"My mom doesn't need your magic sprinkles," Emersen interrupted. "Her pie is perfect just the way it is!" Emersen put her arm around the queen and lead her up the stairs.

"Yes, no thank you!" the queen shouted back to the woman before carrying on inside. "Thanks, honey," she said to Princess Emersen with a smile.

Inside, the queen set her pie on stage and stood next to it. The king, the princess, and Grandma all took their seats in the audience. One by one, the judges tasted the cakes, pies, and cookies. Then it was time to announce the winner.

"Ladies and gentlemen," the announcer said loudly, "please put your hands together for this year's Queen's Baking Competition winner, Her Royal Highness, Queen Kelly!"

The queen had won! The audience cheered and clapped loudly for her.

"I knew she would win," the king whispered to Princess Emersen with a wink.

As they were leaving the building, a poster hanging on the wall caught the princess's eye.

"Kids' Baking Competition" it read. *Hmm,* thought Emersen. "Maybe I should enter," she said out loud, pointing to the poster.

"Of course you should," said the queen. "You know, it's not about winning," she added. "I felt like a winner before the competition had even started."

And they lived happily ever after.

THE END.

Printed in Canada